# The Ginger Ninja

## Three's a Crowd

### Shoo Rayner

a division of Hodder Headline plc

First published in Great Britain in 1997
by Hodder Children's Books



ISBN 0340 69380 0

10 9 8 7 6 5 4 3 2 1



A Catalogue record for this book is available from the British Library

Printed and bound in Great Britain by
Cox & Wyman Ltd, Reading, Berks.

## *Chapter 1*

There is always a disco at St Felix's School before the end of term, and the kittens get very excited, but Ginger gets the most excited of all.

Ginger is pretty good at doing most things, so his friends called him the Ginger Ninja.

This term Ginger's class had been chosen to decorate the school hall.

As Ginger is the best climber in his class, he had been given the job of tying up streamers in the middle of the hall.

Doesn't it look great?
MUNCHTIME DISCO
Yeah! Can't wait for tonight.
My mum's bought me a new bow to wear tonight.

In the evening the kittens arrived for the disco all neatly groomed, and very excited. In the hall, lights flashed in time with the music. The beat was so loud it made their whiskers curl.

Muncher's dad ran the disco and his mum was there to show the kittens how to do some of the dances.

Tonight there was a brand new dance to learn.

In no time at all the whole school had got the hang of it.

Shake that tail,
Bang that nail,
Write me a letter...
...and put it in the mail!

In the middle of the song Ginger pretended to play the guitar.

Even after the disco had finished the kittens didn't stop. Most of them carried on singing all the way home and into bed.

## *Chapter 2*

The next day was the last day of term. The playground was full of kittens doing the Kool Cats song.

Ginger was there, too, pretending to play the guitar part.

The rest of the kittens carried on until the bell rang to start their last day.

In assembly, the Headmaster made a speech and gave prizes to kittens that had tried hard that term.

And then . . .

As a special treat Hilda is going to play to us on her cello... ah yes, a piece of music by Furré called 'Aprés un rave'.
Er... thankyou, Hilda.
Yawn!
Ho hum!

Hilda shuffled
her tail . . .

. . . checked
that her music
was safely on
the stand . . .

. . . tapped
her feet
three times . . .

. . . and launched
into the music.

Ginger was enchanted. Hilda could have been playing specially for him. The music swirled round the hall like a warm summer breeze. He could almost smell the new mown hay and feel the sun shining down on his face.

And yet there was something so sad about the music. Ginger's eyes filled with tears and he didn't really know why.

But he knew that in Hilda's paws, the cello seemed to come alive.

Hilda finished with a great sweep of her bow. Ginger leapt to his feet, clapping and cheering.

Horror of horrors! The whole school turned and looked at Ginger. He was the only one clapping! A million thoughts rushed through his head.

Clap! Clap! Clap!

Ginger held his head up and carried on clapping until the rest of the school joined in.

Ginger winked at Hilda, and she smiled back.

## *Chapter 3*

At breaktime, Ginger followed Hilda into the playground.

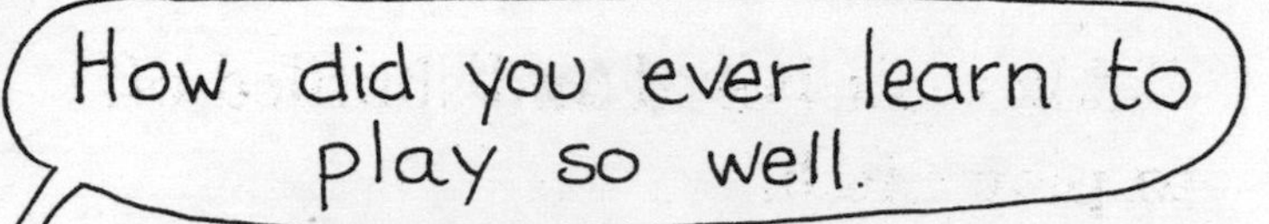
How did you ever learn to play so well.

Well, my dad *is* the School Music Teacher! We're just a very musical family. I've always played music as long as I can remember. I can play the violin and piano too.
Yawn!

Tiddles got bored and shuffled off to play catch.

At the end of the day, the excited kittens rushed out of school to start their holidays. Tiddles bounced up to Ginger.

On the way to Hilda's house
Ginger wondered what it was
like to have a teacher for a dad.

Hilda's dad wasn't an old grump. In fact he was in a very good, holiday mood.

He picked up
his guitar and
tried a few notes.

Then he started to play.
It was the Kool Cats song.

Ginger was so excited he wanted
to play it there and then.

Could you show me how to do that? We've got a guitar at home... well, it's not very good... it's my dad's, but I can ask him... It's only got three strings and it's a bit bashed, but I could–
Woah! One step at a time. It's hard work learning to play an instrument. I wish all my pupils were as keen as you. Bring your dad's guitar round and we'll have a look at it.

When he got home, Ginger asked his dad if he could borrow his guitar.

That night Ginger cuddled his guitar in bed, and dreamed he was a pop star.

## *Chapter 4*

The next morning was the first day of the holidays. Tiddles came round to see if Ginger wanted to play.

Mr Amadeus was surprised to see Tiddles.

Mr Amadeus
picked up Ginger's
guitar. He and
Hilda had a
good look at it.

Mr Amadeus took
the three remaining
strings off the Guitar.

Then he gave
it a really
good polish.

He did something
with a spanner
that made a
terrible creak.

He scraped some
parts with a
special knife and
padded other parts
with tiny bits
of paper.

He oiled the
tuning bits . . .

. . . and carefully
put on a new
set of strings.

Getting it in tune was painful.

Ginger was fascinated. It sounded like a real guitar. Tiddles got very bored.

Mr Amadeus drew four pictures on a piece of paper.

Mr Amadeus helped Ginger to put his paws in the right place.

## *Chapter 5*

Tiddles started to get very lonely over the holidays. He had other friends to play with, but Ginger was his best friend.

Ginger never seemed to be at home.

If he *was* at home he was practising.

Tiddles started sulking.

Even when school started again
Ginger was always busy.

After school he would go to Hilda's house to learn new tunes.

Tiddles sulked even more.

He said unkind things about Hilda, loud enough so that Ginger could hear.

He pinned notes up
around the school.

Ginger got very cross.

Tiddles was furious. He glared at Ginger and Hilda during lessons.

He yawned loudly when they answered questions.

Then he started hitting things.

He hit doors . . .

. . . and dustbins . . .

. . . and desks . . .

. . . and chairs . . .

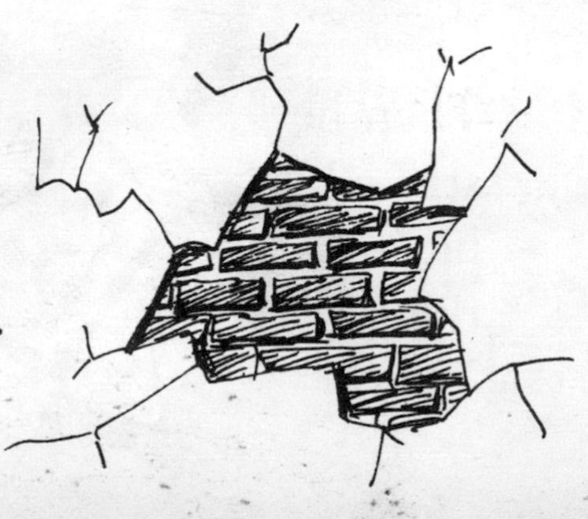

. . . and walls.

He nearly hit Ginger.

Miss Tiffany, their Teacher, knew something was wrong. Ginger and Tiddles had always been friends. Now they wouldn't speak to each other.

Tiddles spent a large part of each lesson drumming his paws on his desk. Miss Tiffany thought it was time to take action . . .

## *Chapter* 6

Tiddles thought he was in big trouble as he followed Miss Tiffany towards the Headmaster's Office.

But she went past the door and on to the music room.

Mr Amadeus, Tiddles needs to let off a bit of steam. He's been bashing and crashing around all week. Do you think you can help?
I think so. Leave him with me, Miss Tiffany, I'll soon sort him out.

Hilda and Ginger were on their way to ask Mr Amadeus if she could go round to Ginger's house.

As they walked towards the music room, an almighty din started up.

They hurried inside and there, banging away on a drum kit, like a wild and crazy kitten, was Tiddles!

Bing
bong
Bash!

When he had worn himself out Hilda rushed over and hugged him.

Tiddles! That was great. A bit on the loud side, but you really can play the drums. You're a natural.
You're right, Hilda, I think we've discovered a hidden talent.
Shucks!
!

## *Chapter 7*

Hilda got Ginger and Tiddles organised. She even taught Tiddles to play gently.

Hilda would then play along on the piano or the cello or the violin.

Shuffa
Bush-bush
Chunka Chung
Waah-eee-ooo-waah-
fiddly-diddly-dee
eee

Tiddles was soon back to his old self again. The band practised and practised until they were good enough to play at the next end of term disco.

Their band was a huge success. And there was one song that they had to play again and again.

Scratch your claws!
Bang those doors!
Twiddle your whiskers with your paws!
Shake that tail!

Bang that nail!
Write me a letter...
... Put it in the mail!
Ooooooh! I just love this guitar bit
Twingle-Twangle-Twong!
Totally awesome!

## ORDER FORM

| | | |
|---|---|---|
| 0 340 61955 4 | The Ginger Ninja | ❑ |
| 0 340 61956 2 | The return of Tiddles | ❑ |
| 0 340 61957 0 | The Dance of the Apple Dumplings | ❑ |
| 0 340 61958 9 | St Felix for the Cup | ❑ |
| 0 340 69379 7 | World Cup Winners | ❑ |
| 0 340 69380 0 | Three's a Crowd | ❑ |

*If you enjoyed this book, you may wish to read more about Ginger's adventures. The Ginger Ninja books are available at your local bookshop or newsagent, or may be ordered direct from the publisher. Just tick the titles you want and fill in the form below. Prices and availability subject to change without notice.*

Write to: Hodder Children's Books, Cash Sales Department, Bookpoint, 39 Milton Park Abingdon, Oxon. OX14 4TD, UK.
If you have a credit card you may order by telephone – 012345 831700.

Please enclose a cheque or postal order made payable to Bookpoint Ltd to the value of the cover price and allow the following for postage and packing: UK & BFPO – £1.00 for the first book, 50p for the second book, and 30p for each additional book ordered up to a maximum charge of £3.00.
OVERSEAS & EIRE – £2.00 for the first book, £1.00 for the second book, and 50p for each additional book.

Name.............................................................................................
Address.........................................................................................
.....................................................................................................
.....................................................................................................

If you would prefer to pay by credit card, please complete:
Please debit my Visa/Access/Diner's Card/American Express (delete as applicable) card no:

| | | | | | | | | | | | | | | | |
|---|---|---|---|---|---|---|---|---|---|---|---|---|---|---|---|
| | | | | | | | | | | | | | | | |

Signature......................................................................................
Expiry Date...................................................................................